Nick and Nack Build a Birdhouse

By Brandon Budzi
Art by Adam Record

HIGHLIGHTS PRESS
Honesdale, Pennsylvania

Stories + Puzzles = Reading Success!

Dear Parents,

Highlights Puzzle Readers are an innovative approach to learning to read that combines puzzles and stories to build motivated, confident readers.

Developed in collaboration with reading experts, the stories and puzzles are seamlessly integrated so that readers are encouraged to read the story, solve the puzzles, and then read the story again. This helps increase vocabulary and reading fluency and creates a satisfying reading experience for any kind of learner. In addition, solving Hidden Pictures puzzles fosters important reading and learning skills such as:

- shape and letter recognition
- letter-sound relationships
- visual discrimination
- logic
- flexible thinking
- sequencing

With high-interest stories, humorous characters, and trademark puzzles, Highlights Puzzle Readers offer a winning combination for inspiring young learners to love reading.

This is Nick.

This is Nack.

Nick loves to **make** things.
Nack loves to **find** things.
They make a good **team**.

You can help them by solving the **Hidden Pictures** puzzles.

"Wait!" says Nack.
"Where are the birds?"
Help Nick and Nack.
Find 5 birds hidden in the picture.
28
29

Happy reading!

It is a hot day.

Nick and Nack eat ice pops.

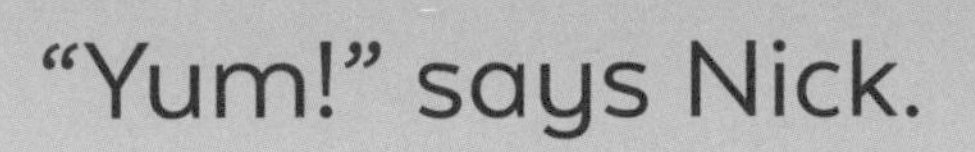

“Yum!” says Nick.

“Yum!” says Nack.

They lick the ice pops.

One lick. Two licks.

More licks. All done!

Now they each have a stick.

“What can we do with the sticks?”

asks Nack.

“We can make a birdhouse,”

says Nick.

“How can we make a birdhouse?”

asks Nack.

"First, we need more sticks,"

says Nick.

“I can help find more sticks,”

says Nack.

"Yum!" says Nick.

He eats two ice pops.

"Yum!" says Nack.

He eats the rest.

"Now we need paint," says Nick.

"I can help find paint," says Nack.

Nick finds yellow paint.

Nack finds red paint.

“We can use both!” says Nick.

“What can we use to paint?”

asks Nack.

“We can use paintbrushes,”

says Nick.

Help Nick and Nack.

Find 5 paintbrushes hidden in the picture.

GLUE

“Now we need glue,” says Nick.

“I can help find glue,” says Nack.

Nick looks on the shelf under the window.

Nack looks on the shelf over the window.

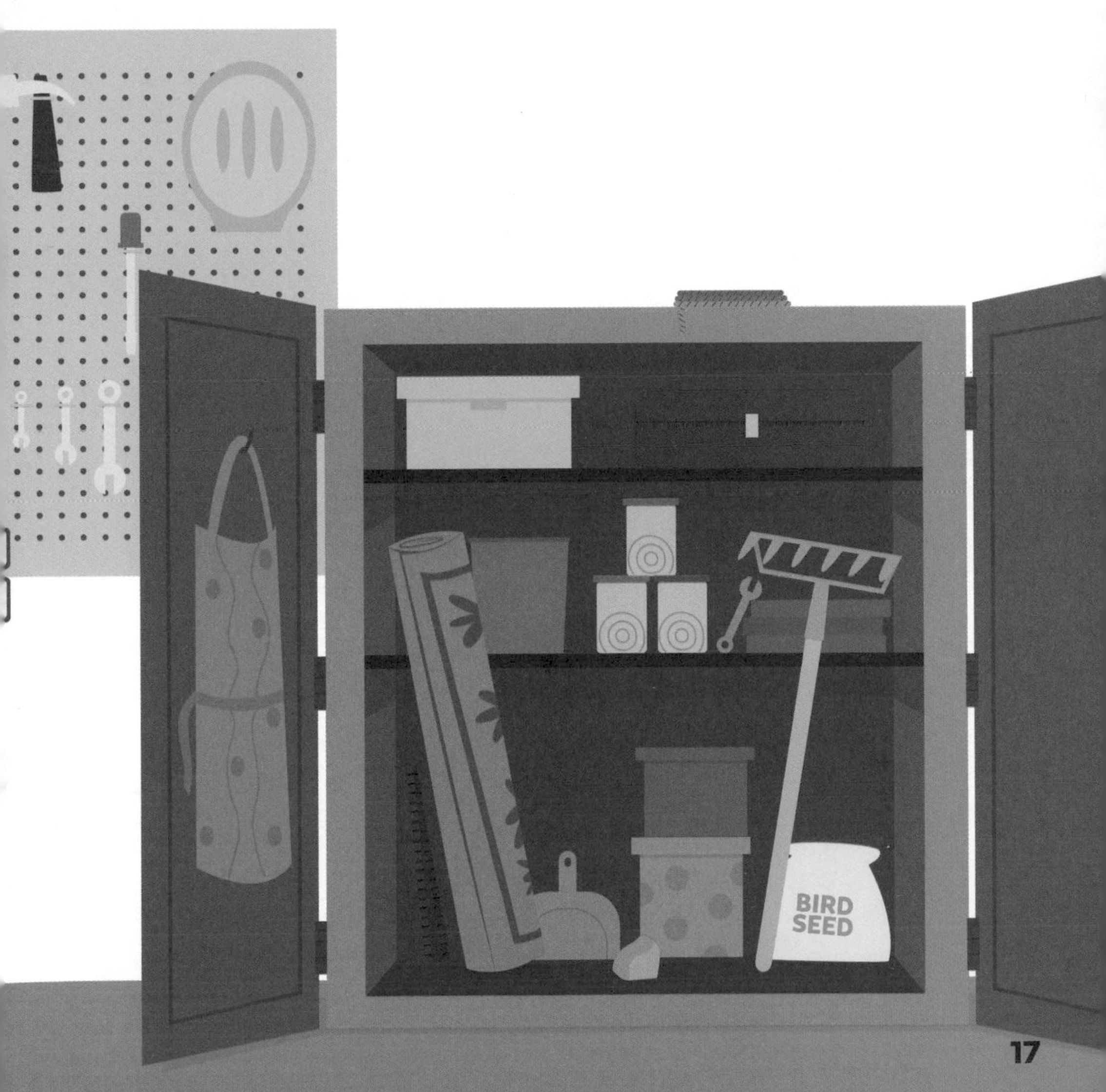

"I found the glue!" says Nack.

"We can use the glue to put the birdhouse together," says Nick.

"Can we also use tape?" asks Nack.

"Yes!" says Nick.

Help Nick and Nack.

Find 5 rolls of tape hidden in the picture.

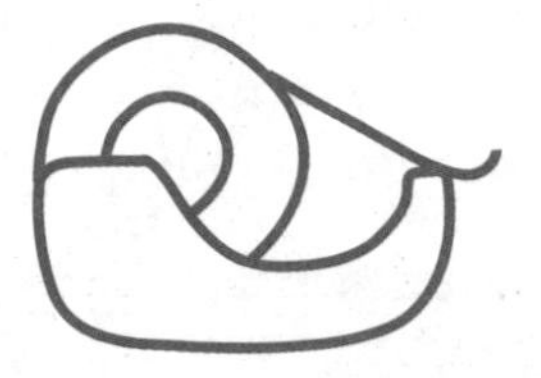

GLUE

"Now we need rope," says Nick.

"I can help find rope," says Nack.

Nack finds a rake.

He finds a rock.

He finds a rug.

He cannot find rope.

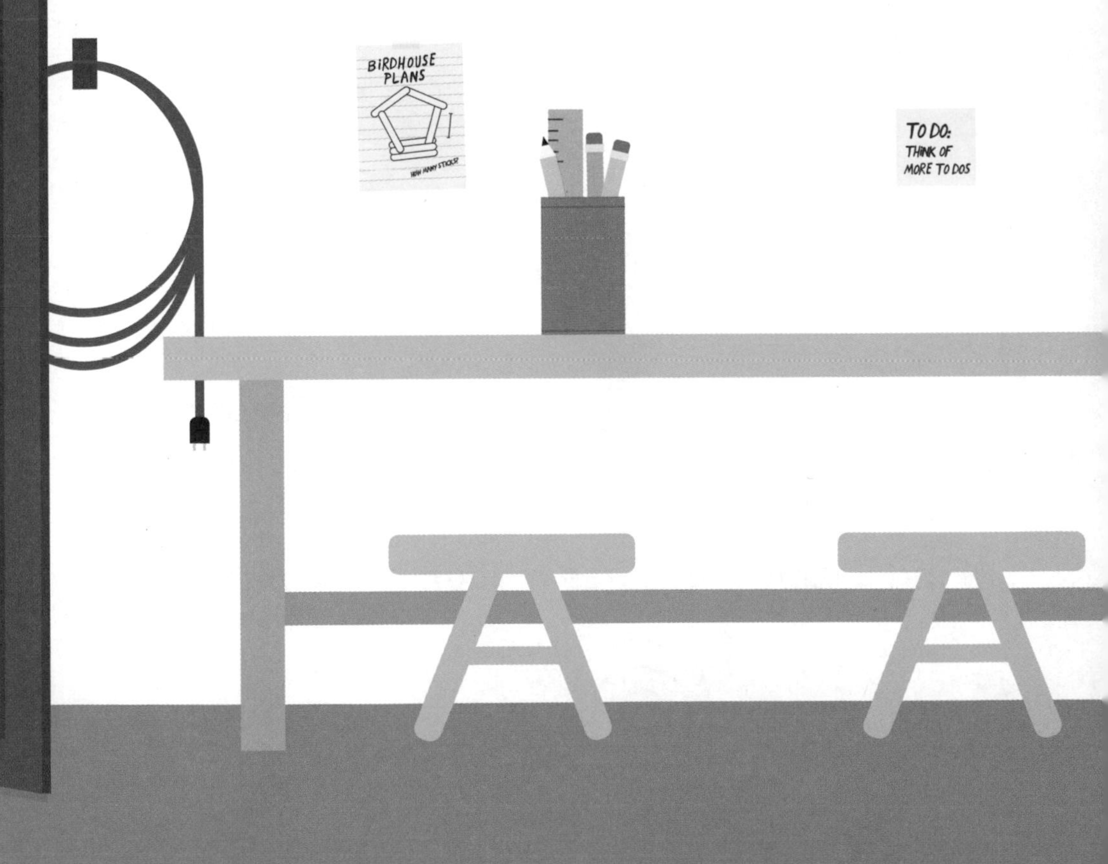

“Here is the rope!” says Nack.

“How much rope do we need?”

“We need three feet,” says Nick.

“We can use a tape measure.”

Help Nick and Nack.

Find 5 tape measures hidden in the picture.

BIRD
SEED

“Now let’s build a birdhouse!” says Nick.

“Hooray!” says Nack.

They glue the sticks together.

They paint the birdhouse.

BIRDHOUSE PLANS
BIRD SEED

They hang the birdhouse.

“I like our birdhouse,” says Nick.

“I like our birdhouse, too,”
says Nack.

“Will the birds like it?” asks Nick.

“Wait!” says Nack.

“Where are the birds?”

Help Nick and Nack.

Find 5 birds hidden in the picture.

Build Your Own BIRDHOUSE!

WHAT YOU NEED:

- Craft sticks
- Glue
- Tape or clips
- Yarn or rope

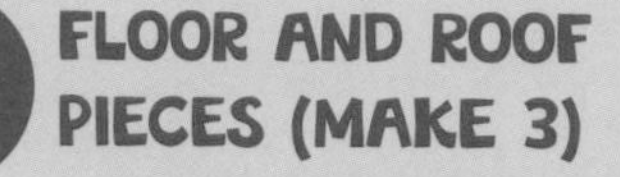

1 FLOOR AND ROOF PIECES (MAKE 3)

- Line up 12 sticks.
- Glue a stick across the top.
- Glue a stick across the bottom.

Let the glue dry before you pick up the pieces.

2 SIDES (MAKE 2)

- Glue 5 sticks together as shown.
- Glue 5 more sticks on top of the first layer.

3 PUT THEM TOGETHER

- Glue the 2 sides to the floor.
- Glue each roof piece to the top.

Use clips or tape to hold the pieces while they dry.

4 FINISH IT UP

- Glue more craft sticks to the sides to make walls.
- Glue a craft stick on top of the roof.
- Add a hanger.

You can paint your birdhouse any color you want. Or you can leave it plain.

Nick and Nack's TIPS

- Gather your supplies before you start crafting.
- Ask an adult or robot for help with anything sharp or hot.
- Clean up your workspace when your craft is done.

Published by Highlights Press
815 Church Street
Honesdale, Pennsylvania 18431
ISBN (paperback): 978-1-68437-932-3
ISBN (hardcover): 978-1-68437-984-2
ISBN (ebook): 978-1-64472-224-4

Library of Congress Control Number: 2019940915
Printed in Melrose Park, IL, USA
Mfg. 02/2020

First edition
Visit our website at Highlights.com.
10 9 8 7 6 5 4 3 2 1

Photos by Jim Filipski, Guy Cali Associates, Inc.

This book has been officially leveled by using the F&P Text Level Gradient™ Leveling System.

For assistance in the preparation of this book, the editors would like to thank Vanessa Maldonado, MSEd, MS Literacy Ed. K–12, Reading/LA Consultant Cert., K–5 Literacy Instructional Coach; and Gina Shaw.